William Ayres Armstrong

Miracle Hill

A Legendary Tale Of Wisconsin

William Ayres Armstrong

Miracle Hill
A Legendary Tale Of Wisconsin

ISBN/EAN: 9783743351158

Manufactured in Europe, USA, Canada, Australia, Japa

Cover: Foto ©Andreas Hilbeck / pixelio.de

Manufactured and distributed by brebook publishing software
(www.brebook.com)

William Ayres Armstrong

Miracle Hill

MIRACLE HILL.

A LEGENDARY TALE OF WISCONSIN.

———

BY W. A. ARMSTRONG.

ILLUSTRATED.

MILWAUKEE, WIS.:
CRAMER, AIKENS & CRAMER, ENGRAVERS AND PRINTERS.
1889.

Through the instrumentality of one who revered the place, and believed in its mysteries, I visited the spot; and to her I respectfully dedicate this book.

THE AUTHOR.

MIRACLE HILL.

PART FIRST.

Introductory.

THIS waif of the pen is launched upon the sea of literature, freighted with impressions lingering in the memory of the writer after repeated visits to a remarkable place.

When the notes for the work were taken, the intention of the writer was to publish a journalistic sketch, and embellish it by photography from the scenes that lend enchantment to a place almost unknown to the outside world.

As the task progressed, the importance of the subject became more apparent, which led him to change the plan of publication to one permitting a portrayal of greater detail, and one allowing a wider range for the writer's conception of the beauties pervading the theme.

The principal aim of the writer will be to embody the pages with truth, and while his pen threads the dominion of thought the atmosphere of reality that it floats in will entertain, if it does not instruct.

There will be no effort made to convert the reader to the belief that animates the people who worship at the shrine written of. The subject will be viewed from an unbiased standpoint, and treated with a tinge of reverence, prompted by the wonders the place had the power to inspire.

If allowed to speak in general terms of the church, much could be written to interest those concerned in church matters that others might deem irrelevant to this subject; still, the writer feels like adding occasional notes, even at the risk of appearing digressive.

The church has contributed food to the brain of all ages, and it will continue a topic of conjecture in all time to come. In the astonishingly rapid growth of this country it has been the great landmark of progress, their white spires have shone in the moonlight by the side of every public highway, and their shadows were obliquely cast over graves reached only by the depths of some lonely country lane.

The tendency of the church is to support the infirm ; depravity may seek the shelter of its wing to hide iniquity, but it does not prevent church influences from sustaining the weak.

The church is the carpenter of character and the joiner of sentiment; it frames an every-day life to fit a spiritual existence.

Though not always in immediate sympathy with those who surround it, a church invariably exercises a wholesome influence over the community in which it exists.

An hour spent in an old Quaker meeting-house was more instructive than the best day the writer ever spent in school; the bowed forms of mute worshipers, immovable in silent prayer, though speechless, unfolded pages of tender suggestions that never were forgotten.

The children who grow up around an out of the way church may, through the influence of parentage, be skeptical of the precepts expounded from the pulpit, but they never forget the lesson of respect inculcated through the mediumship of the green mounds and white headstones that embellish its silent old graveyard.

It was chance that directed the writer's attention to this subject, yet investigation disclosed things that were strange, and beliefs entirely new to him. There arose so many varied points to add to the interest of the subject, that he wondered why, through the enterprise of journalism, it had not been the recipient of greater publicity before.

While the legendary history of this resort is known to a comparative few, its more meritorious claims are recognized by people living a great distance away, and if the reader will follow the details of this book, he will find proofs of the sincerity of the writer's opinion.

The spot has within itself the elements to foster

romance or inspire belief, and if robbed of the phases that attract the pious devotee, it still is resplendent in secular beauty. It is unique in scenery, and weird in tradition ; and while its simplicity charms, its quietness soothes.

Unlike any other place, this has had no ambitious prospects, or spur of moneyed expectations to advance its interests. It never courted notoriety, or shunned investigation. It quietly bore the odium of envy and the ridicule of disbelief. It passed through all the different periods of probation. It was stranded on the shoals of poverty, and floated with the tide of thrift. It drifted, in simplicity, from the old year to the new, with no ostentation, without effort, yet, by its unobtrusion, secured public confidence and commanded respect.

In his search for information the author has driven to this spot in all seasons of the year. Spring, summer, autumn and winter alike have found him jogging over some of the hilly roads leading to the place, and he never made the journey without feeling amply compensated for the fatigue it was necessary to incur. The more he investigated the peculiarities of the neighborhood, the more he found that his pen was inadequate to perform the task required of it, and the more he saw, the more he felt incompetent to do the subject justice.

This theme is one to awaken the tender susceptibilities of youth without infringing upon the biased opinions

A Spring Scene Close to the Entrance, Miracle Hill.

of age, and it is more than likely it will interest some treading the declivity that gently nears the end. People in all ages, and in all conditions of life, long for mysticism. Who is there but can remember how in childhood he listened eagerly to catch the details of a fireside story of a weird performance? And to-day, if his eye, in the reading of current events, alights upon an item bordering on a mystery, it produces about the same effect.

In the search for particulars for this work, the writer was favorably impressed by the apparent truthfulness of those interviewed, and the sincerity of others making their pilgrimages to the church. The skeptic will doubt and the scoffer may scorn the tales that fall from the lips of those strong in the belief of the cures brought about by a stay at this place; but no argument, however logical, will shake the faith of those journeying here for prayer.

The illustrations that embellish this little book are the best that money could procure. The scenes are real, and were obtained in detail by the author, with care, for this work. Great pains were taken in the selection of the views to combine the real with the writer's conception of the ideal. How well he succeeded is left entirely to the judgment of those who peruse these pages.

The story of the hermit of the hill, given as received, is from the most authentic source at present obtainable, making all due allowance for the vagaries of years and the ever-changing memories of men.

The history of the church and its origin is told as it was gleaned from the Vicar-General of the diocese, Mgr. Batz, and the pastor of the Arch-Diocese, who has officiated on its feast days for years, and who kindly aided in procuring much valuable information.

AN EARTH-CUT ON THE ASCENT.

PART SECOND.

The Legend of St. Mary's Hill.

MANY years ago a farmer, whose home was among the hills, was returning from the neighboring village of Hartford, late at night. The round, full moon had just risen, and as he approached Saint Mary's Hill from the west, that eminence stood in inky blackness between him and the silvery eastern sky. The outline of the hill was as sharply defined as a silhouette, and on the very summit he saw the form of a cross and a kneeling figure. He watched the strange apparition for an hour, when the figure slowly rose and disappeared in the black woods of the hillside.

Not many mornings after he again saw the odd figure on the top of the hill engaged in devotion. The advent of the anchorite soon became generally known in the neighborhood, and his home was discovered in a cave, which he had dug in a gorge, on the east side of the hill.

No one disturbed him. His only occupation seemed to be his pilgrimages to the hill-top to engage in prayer. He gradually became sufficiently familiar with the inhabitants to answer their friendly salutations, and occasionally engaged in religious converse with them. One farmer became his confidant, and to him he related the following history :

His name was Francois Soubrio. He was born some twenty miles from Strasburg, and, being of high birth, was educated for the priesthood. He became enamored of a lady near the monastery where he was pursuing his course of study, and finding his passion reciprocated, renounced his priestly vows and became openly betrothed.

Disgraced in the eyes of his family, and under the ban of the church, he postponed his marriage, and bidding farewell for a season to his affianced, he resolved to banish himself and test the strength of both his own and the lady's affection.

After two years he returned, and it was the same old story of the absent lover and the faithless maid, with a swain ever present to urge his suit. The evidence of their unholy intimacy was so tangible that in a frenzy of despair, urged on by a love now turned to hate, he killed the faithless one and fled.

He again came to America, landing at Quebec, and

became a recluse in one of the monasteries of the quaint old city. Here he remained for years, tortured with remorse for his recreancy to religious vows, and the crime that lay even heavier on his heart. His only relief was in prayer, penance, and delving among the old French manuscripts found in the musty corners of his retreat.

Among them was a partially mutilated diary kept by Jacques Marquette during the summer and fall of 1673, in which was a detailed account of a memorable voyage with Louis Joliet to the Mississippi River, via the Fox and Wisconsin Rivers, returning up the Illinois River and the western coast of Lake Michigan to Green Bay, where the expedition first embarked.

His attention was particularly drawn to an expedition from a creek, where Marquette had landed on his return voyage, a hard day's march west, to a steep and lofty cone-shaped hill, which he climbed to the summit and thereon erected a rude stone altar, raised a cross, dedicated the spot as holy ground forever, in the name of his tutelary saint, Mary, and left it towering in its solitude.

Francois felt that the mission whereby to work out his full atonement was declared to him. On his knees he vowed to rediscover the holy hill and re-erect the long ago moldered cross upon its summit.

From the description of the coast, and a rough map

which was with the manuscript, he had little difficulty in locating the spot.

Arriving in Chicago he was delayed in his journey by a serious illness, which left him a confirmed paralytic, with only a partial use of his limbs. In this crippled condition he at last reached the end of his pilgrimage, and late one evening crawled through the thick wood on his knees to the summit of the hill, where he spent the remainder of the night in prayer to the holy Saint Mary. With the dawn he rose from his knees in all the vigor of his early manhood, his palsy gone, his health restored.

On the spot where his miraculous cure was wrought, he built a rude altar. Every day and night, often twice, sometimes thrice a day he went up to this chapel to offer devotion. So frequent were these pilgrimages that the ceaseless tread of his feet defined the path amid the trees.

As the days merged into months, and the months were lost in years, this pathway widened to an existence that still remains a memento of his early devotion.

Along the path, at regular intervals, he erected rude crosses, before which he knelt on his way to and from the summit of the peak, often doing extreme penance by making the pilgrimage on his bare knees. People from all the country round had heard the wonderful story of his miraculous cure, and numbers sought relief from their bodily ailments through prayer at the hermit's shrine.

For seven years he remained in the vicinity, living in the little hut, whose primitive condition is shown in

THE HERMIT'S HUT.

detail by the picture, made ere it was stricken by the blight of decay. Backed by the thick wood, its gable and front was adorned by a nude figure, emblematic of the belief of its strange occupant. The simplicity of the structure was in accordance with the primeval character of the place, while the cross, all potent in the faith, stood prominent in the foreground. The cross, still leaning, exists; but the cabin, like the hermit, has disappeared—the one by the natural process of decay, the other in mystery, as a light that glimmers to guide the mariner on a rock-bound coast dies out without reason, so he went out in the labyrinth of the world, without cause.

A rumor was current that he was seen since, but it was never authentically verified. We leave him to his wanderings. Tradition says his apparition is sometimes seen in the dusk of evening kneeling at one of the brown crosses along his old path, or gliding in and out of the chapel, where the sacred relics of his early shrine are still kept.

PART THIRD.

The Charms That Enlist Our Attention.

IN Wisconsin, less than two hours' ride from the metropolis of the State, are a hill, a church and a neighborhood famed far and near as the birth-place of miracles. Here, through the invisible power of the place alone, it is claimed, have marvelous cures been perfected, and for thirty years the wonderful tales have been growing in number and in interest. The illustrations that embellish these pages are from photographs made on the spot, and the view of the chapel shows leaning against its columns the time-worn crutches discarded by the pilgrims who to-day are living proofs of the miracles performed, whether by faith alone or by the wondrous power of the place, we leave others to judge.

"There are conservative people to whom incredulity is a virtue in the face of all evidence; yet it is unquestionable that the king's touch has cured scrofula. It is undeniable that relics of St. Catharine have cured cancer of the tongue; that an appeal to St. Lucia has cured cataract, and to St. Appollonia toothache. Doctors have

cured without touching the patient. Blue-glass has
overcome serious organic diseases. Faith-healers have
made the lame to walk and the blind to see." Why,
then, we ask in all candor, should the miracles attrib-
uted to this sacred place be questioned? Here is the
quiet that only these surroundings can give. Here are
the bright skies, the pure air, the plain food, and the
exercise, that alone could renew an enervated system.

The place is known by various appellations, but the
usual designation is *Holy Hill.* In the original survey,
the title of Lapham's Peak was given it. Later it was
called Hermit's Hill by the people of the neighborhood,
although the church is known in the diocese as St.
Mary's Help of Christians, probably derived from the
legend that dedicated it to the Blessed Virgin Mary. It
is situated near the town line of Erin, in the County
of Washington, and is the highest point of land in
Eastern Wisconsin, being over eight hundred feet above
the level of Lake Michigan, and thirteen hundred feet
above the level of the sea.

The location is about equally distant from Richfield
and Hartford, stations on the Northern Division of the
Chicago, Milwaukee & St. Paul Railroad. It can be
reached also from Rugby Junction and Schleisingerville,
stations on the Wisconsin Central. The drive is best
from Hartford. The church can be seen from there,
standing in its solitude, eight miles away to the south-
west. It then is a mere speck to the vision, in a setting

of changeable blue. The direction to it that a bird would fly will not cover the round-about road that zig-zags by section lines or school-house corners much farther. A mariner's course is guided by a star; so this church is a fixed point to the eye for quite a distance after leaving Hartford, but lost to sight long before you get there by the crooked route, that, snake-like, bends its way around the intervening hills. A glimpse of it is sometimes caught from the right or left, as the road winds around a prominent spur or climbs a loftier peak, and as the distance diminishes, the interest in the place increases.

"THE FESTIVAL OF THE ASSUMPTION.

" Yesterday, being the festival of Assumption, was celebrated with customary fervor by the faithful at Holy Hill, the noted place of pilgrimage in Washington County.

" Despite the murky atmosphere and oppressive heat the attendance was very large, numbering fully 3,000. People had come not only from the immediate neighborhood but from Chicago, Lake Geneva, Burlington, Franklin, Waterloo, Schleisingerville, Hartford, Beaver Dam, Fox Lake and this city. Father Fessler, president of Pio Nono College, St. Francis, arrived at an early hour to hear confession, reading mass at 9 o'clock.

" Immediately thereafter confessions were continued before four more priests until the celebration of high mass, at which the Rt. Rev. Vicar-General Batz officiated, assisted by Fathers Fessler and Weyer, the Vicar-General and Father Fessler delivering the sermons in English and German respectively. There were some 160 communicants, who had come to seek relief. The ceremony is said to have been an exceedingly impressive one."

The above clipping from the Milwaukee *Daily Sentinel* of August the 16th, 1888, is introduced here to show the deep interest people living at a distance take in this place. On the afternoon of August 14th, the writer took his chances on a crowded train to attend the interesting meeting just referred to. Arriving at Richfield, an hour later, the conveyances were inadequate to the task of transportation, unless willing to ride unprotected in a drizzling rain. Subsequent information reported, "besides those sleeping in the church, at least forty could find no accommodations."

Reliable people, who have resided almost in the shadows of this peak for twenty-five years, claim to tell only what they can substantiate with proofs. They say the cures here are attributable solely to the merits of the place; but as it is not within the province of the writer to discuss this question, he will confine himself to a narrative description of the church, the neighborhood, and the predominating attractions that lure the visitant to the spot.

The location of the property is in the midst of a

territory that is wild by nature, and subdued only by toil and perseverance. The hills still rise in their pristine grandeur, yet the slopes are rich with verdure that feed the wandering flocks. The place has no dizzy heights to peer over, or rock-faced cliffs to scale; yet the rugged look on the face suggests a power, all unseen.

It is entirely free from the turmoil that pervades the busy haunts of men. The smoke from a workshop never dimmed the rarity of the atmosphere, nor have the echoes from a locomotive whistle ever disturbed the dream of its solitude. The entire country that surrounds the church is exceedingly uneven, when viewed from any of the elevated points of observation. Every approach is beset with steep hills, and as you attain an eminence there is always something novel in the gully below. A few tenantless cabins are scattered in the vicinity that give a glimpse of desolation in a land of milk and honey. The little patches that surround these structures are symbols of ruin, the briars and brambles vie for priority, or rule by an abundance that strives to overwhelm.

With all the ups and downs that the face of this country presents, there still are many thrifty people engaged in the husbandry of these rough acres. They are generally of foreign extraction and, with primitive habits, prosper, while those to the manor born might fail. They seem satisfied with their mode of life, and have a notable reverence for the miraculous hill, and the legends pertaining to it.

If a being could be spirited to this spot in a dream, and, like Rip Van Winkle, awake to reality at a season when all nature was in the full flush of her most enchanting power, his surprise would be equally astounding. After the first frosts of an autumn foreboding has changed the color of the leaves, the scene beggars description. The foliage then assumes the brightest attire ever donned by nature, and every twig is radiant in its holiday garb. A level acre is not within the radius of the eye, and every peak and indenture has some tree or bush thrown in relief by a contrast of gayety. All the varied hues indigenous to this lovely spot greet the eye with delight in endless confusion. The knobs are resplendent with beams from hard wood leaves, while the slopes sink meltingly subdued until they are indefinably lost in the deep red of the sumac that fringes the bottom.

The church is a conspicuous object to all the neighboring country. Its elevated position enables the residents within a radius of ten miles to point the stranger with pride to the " Church of Miracles." The swain who treads the furrow in the wake of his plow, and the maid who chirps her song at milking time, both pause in their task to look at this beacon of hope.

As I viewed it from the valley upon one of its unapproachable sides, a feeling of veneration, akin to awe,

An Autumnal View of the Church.

crept over me. Upon a cone-shaped peak, almost circular in form, and thickly covered to its base with rocks and tough timber, stood the church.

As a landmark to guide, and an emblem of faith, it is strikingly beautiful and prominently alone. Its gold cross glistens in the bright summer sun, and trembles like the stricken deer in the rude winter wind. All through the long day, and deep in the dark night, like a sentinel to guard the weird mysteries, it keeps the lonely watch; and when the shadows of evening spread their misty mantle of dew, it towers there still, in its isolated solitude.

It is the only place of the kind on this vast continent. The story of the hermit dates the consecration as holy ground back to 1673—over two hundred years. It was dedicated then to the tutelage of the Blessed Mary, and it remains after two centuries, with growing popularity, devoted to the same purposes. No parochial duties were ever performed in its sanctuary; no hands clasped in wedlock or hearts bound in fear. No funeral procession has ever wended the way to its portals, or burial service been read from its altar, and it is the only church in the Catholic faith that is devoid of that quaint emblem of mortality, a grave-yard. Nowhere in the range of vision are the white stones that call up the goblins of retrospection.

The knob, or peak, upon which the church is built, is just large enough to leave a walk around it. From this walk there is an extended view for many miles in every direction. The spires of half a dozen other churches (as beacons of faith), in the distance, point heavenward, and on a bright, clear spring day the white sails of vessels are discernable thirty miles to the east on the great inland sea. The spire of St. Augustine is seen in the east, St. Patrick in the west, St. Killian in the northeast, a little north of east St. John's, due north twelve miles in the distance is St. Lawrence, while southeast stands St. Mary's of Richfield.

PART FOURTH.

The Growth of the Church.

ABOUT forty years ago, Dr. Paulhuber became the owner of the Hill property, and on the eve of departure for Europe he donated it to the Arch-Diocese of Milwaukee. By law the property after Paulhuber's transfer was not taxable. It happened that the property adjoining was sold for taxes, and by mistake the deed was made to cover the hill property. This error encumbered it. The Vicar-General assumed the responsibility, and cleared its title, the money being raised by contribution. One enthusiastic individual made his will in favor of the church, and from that will the diocese realized four thousand dollars.

Many years ago, Father J. B. Haslbaum was instrumental in the erection of a cross upon the summit of the hill. The man who is entitled to the credit of putting it in place still lives within the shadow of the peak. What memories must cluster in the brain of a man who has seen the frosts of forty winters gather in this vicinity!

In the year 1861, the Rev. George Strickner, then

pastor of St. Boniface, now in his private retreat at Sheboygan, encouraged by the neighbors residing in the vicinity, assisted in building the first rude chapel. It was erected on an elevation twenty feet higher than the present summit, which had to be cut down from its cone-shaped pinnacle to get ground room in length and breadth for the present more commodious edifice.

It was on the twenty-fourth day of May, 1863, that the first procession wended its way up a narrow path, almost enclosed by shrubbery and underbrush, to the top of the hill, where the little chapel was blessed, and the first sermon was preached from the threshold of a rude hut to a multitude that had gathered and densely covered every available spot. How the people got the material for this structure into place is still an enigma, as the logs had to be carried up on the shoulders of men.

The Reverend Ferdinand Raes, when pastor of Richfield, took charge of the hill, and at regular intervals held divine service there. Finding that the little chapel would not accommodate the many pilgrims, he, with the consent of Archbishop Henni, commenced the present structure, for which he took up collections in a number of parishes in the Arch-Diocese.

The corner-stone of the present edifice was laid in 1879, and the church was formally dedicated in 1882, being three years in building. The cost of the church has been very great in proportion to the simplicity of its unfinished interior. The brick were made at the foot of the hill, and cost thirteen dollars a thousand, which added greatly to the expense of the structure; and it must have been a Herculean task to get the material to the summit to finish it.

It is now maintained entirely by the contributions of the pilgrims. As a place of pilgrimage it is more attractive without a resident pastor, and it is presided over on feast-days generally by the Rt. Rev. Vicar-Gen'l Batz, of Milwaukee. All neighboring priests, in good standing, are welcome to officiate, and they cheerfully do so when called upon.

There are certain days for solemn services, at which there is always a large attendance.

May the twenty-fourth is the titular feast of the church, termed the "Feast of St. Mary's Help of Christians."

June the seventeenth, the "Feast of the Sacred Heart of Jesus."

July the second, the "Feast of Visitation of the Blessed Virgin."

August the fifteenth, the "Feast of the Assumption," always a day of holy obligations, and largely attended.

September the eighth, the "Feast of the Nativity."

October, as a rule the day following the first Sunday, "Feast of the Solemnity of the Holy Rosary."

The attendance on feast-days in good weather is always large. Two thousand people frequently attend services at one time. The religious character of the place exercises a strange power and a soothing influence over its visitants. Many " who go to scoff, remain to pray."

At intervals there are other devotional exercises by different priests, but the above are stated services and under control at present of the Rev. N. M. Zimmer, of Hartford, whose picture, accompanying this sketch is from a photograph made a few days before the publication of this work.

THE APPROACH FROM HARTFORD.

PART FIFTH.

Strange Facts, and Pleasant Fancies.

" The sun had just reached out and kissed
The tree tops, from his cowl of mist ;
And, spreading far as eye could gaze,
There rose a tender sea of haze,
That made the landscape dim, but fair,
As gauze more sweet makes pictures rare."
—*Mrs. Cornie Law, St. John.*

AS the traveler approaches the Miracle Grounds by the road from Hartford, the church lies off directly to the right, across the intervening fields and foot-hills, less than a mile away. Looking up the rise of the roadway, the carriage going over the brow of the hill is on a direct line between the church and the old log house that is pictured on another page. Just over the top of this little rise, and to the right, within fifty feet of where the carriage is seen, there is a gate, the first gate that admits the visitor to the hallowed precincts made sacred through the dedication of a peak, by an old French missionary, two hundred and fifteen years ago.

Upon those deeply tinged with susceptibility proximity to this consecrated spot exerts a subtle influence. Being preoccupied with thoughts pertaining to the strange tales and weird illusions that cluster so thickly around the place, the writer drove listlessly past the plain barred entrance gate that is hardly perceptible on the approach from the west. The day was new, the air was sweet as baby's breath; yet, oblivious to all, in a phantasy of meditation, his brain was fraught with the mystic imaginings, entitled—

A DREAM OF THE MOMENT.

Visions of cripples in helpless infirmity,
  Toiling to get to this Mecca of prayer;
Forms that were fashioned by kinks of
    adversity,
  Figures with energy born of despair.

Eyes that were sightless, and steps of
    uncertainty,
  Looks that appealed to a heart made of stone;
Tears that could play on the lute strings of sympathy,
  Chords that since childhood had slumbered un-
    known.

The long line of spectres grew
    dim in the distance,
  Still there were others just
    rounding to view.
As bubbles that germ in the
  foam of a breaker
  Their forms were as odd as
    their phases were new.

A thin mist obscures the expanse of an ocean,
  A cloud intervening will cut off the sun.
So thus, when I sought to hold closer communion,
  The phantoms receded. the vision had flown.

ENTRANCE TO THE MEADOW, AND CHURCH AS SEEN FROM THERE.

The first entrance gate is on the side of a gentle declivity, and almost directly in front of a quaint looking log house that backs against a hill with gable end

A QUAINT HOUSE, NEAR THE ENTRANCE.

to the road. The dilapidated condition of this structure is in marked contrast to the thriftiness of the miracle church property. The prominence of the front of the house, that almost overhangs the roadway, is increased by a board addition that is suspended from the projecting roof, leaving a protruding floor that is reached from the ground by a crude, unenclosed stairway, starting from the ground at the corner of the house, and landing over the basement door in the middle of the overhanging room. The steep slope behind and to the left of the house is covered with a growth of trees and underbrush, while on the opposite side, the gate is attached to a rough split-rail fence, resting on rock boulders, gathered in an early day from what is now a sweet-scented meadow.

From the gate our course was by the confines of this meadow, whose edge is fringed with berry bushes and wild flowers. In the distance could be heard the sound of a mowing machine, while the breeze came fragrant with the delicate odor of fresh-cut hay. This drive ends, amid rocks and stones, in a rough little grove, whose trees cast their shadows almost to the foot of the double picket gate that guards the entrance to the praying ground. An open panel in the fence to the left of this gate shows the road that leads directly on around the base of the spur that forms the pocket of the gorge. This road carries the visitor by the point just described, into the low-land of the meadow, directly underneath the shadow of the church hill, and to the only house of entertainment on the grounds.

Looking beyond the gate, to the left, is seen an iso-

The Picket Gate in Winter.

lated tree. Upon the rock at its root the scribe loitered
in quiet contemplation. The ground to the right was
closely covered with a scrubby growth of underbrush,
topped by a wealth of red sumac. A cut in the earth

A PRAYING STATION—WINTER.

modified the rise as the road curved to the left through
the hill. To the right, on the top of the bank, between
the edge and the rustic rail fence, stood an unpretentious wooden cross, which is the first of the fourteen

praying stations, that have added so much to the celebrity of the place. Around these posts hover the strange traditions and weird suggestions of the dead past, and, like the monitors of a dim past, they line the path from gate to summit. Each is a simple wooden upright crossed by an arm. Above and below the arm at each end are attached half circular blocks, to relieve the plainness. Where the arm is joined to the upright, inserted in the wood, is a small water-color picture, commemorative of some event in the crucifixion, and covered by a glass to protect it from the elements. The crosses are all painted a brown umber color, and at the base of each is a rude foot-stool, made from pine plank, to allow the devotee to kneel in meek supplication. Daily, during propitious seasons, are afflicted people in all stages of decrepitude making the journey to and from the church. They stop to pray, or toil wearily on, as their age or infirmities permit. There have been others who made continued laborious pilgrimages to the place, believing that the greater the amount of suffering they bore, the more certain would be the intercession of the saints for their relief. Some move slowly and on bended knees. It is said that weak and delicate women have made the journey in shotted shoes which bathed their feet in blood; thus emulating the example of the martyrs of old who by their sufferings proved themselves faithfully heroic.

In Jerulasem, about the year 1342, the Friars Minor

of St. Francis—commonly termed the Franciscan monks —were successful in enkindling a veneration for these crosses. They erected stations in their churches to the number of fourteen, which they termed "The Way of the Cross." They represented the path traversed by the Redeemer, laden with his cross, from the house of Pontius Pilate, to Mount Calvary and the Holy Sepulchre. To encourage the faithful to undertake pilgrimages to these sacred places, certain indulgences were granted by the Popes, conditional upon the fulfillment of specific requirements. To gain the indulgences of "The Way of the Cross," it is necessary to go from station to station. It will not suffice to merely look upon the crosses from the same spot. But if, on account of a great crowd, a person could not go from one station to another, it would suffice to kneel and rise to each cross. "The Way of the Cross" can be performed either privately or solemnly in the church where it is established, provided the meditations are sincerely pious on each of the fourteen mysteries.

Climbing the ascent to the first praying station, and turning our back to the cross, we can look through the foliage of the tree near the gate, previously spoken of, to the home of the resident farmer. The buildings here are primitive in their mode of construction. They are all built of logs hewn with an ax, and while unpretentious, are at least substantial. The view is over the picket fence of the garden patch to the back door of the dwelling in the centre of the group. The barn, wagon-house and corn crib are to the right; to the left a low log out-kitchen.

For the next six hundred feet the rise seems like a country road that has turned from the main traveled

HOME OF THE RESIDENT FARMER.

way to some secluded retreat. At this point the road crosses the head of the gorge, where a glance to the left discloses a view that rivals in beauty the splendors of an Alpine prospect. Being at a height to look down upon the house whose hospitality is proverbial, we view with interest the place where the poor and afflicted receive good food, clean beds, and the attention contributed only by good Samaritans without the hope of pecuniary benefit.   In this respect, too, is the place bordering on the miraculous, as, in this State, noted for its summer resorts, there are no others conducted on a principle to give more than they get pay for.

As we gaze from our elevated position, in the foreground, almost beneath our feet, is an unpretentious two-story frame structure upon a firm stone basement. A veranda on the first floor is covered by a roof whose shingles glisten in the sun, while the wind idly flaps the clean linen blinds beneath the half-closed sash.   A serpentine path bends to the left as the gorge widens in the meadow, while a stump, a stack, or a crude fence, breaks the distance in the rolling fields to the east.

A foot-path from the house is intercepted by a rustic fence that marks the boundary line of the cultivated patch that extends up the rise to the road. (See Path from the Meadow, page 55.)   The parallel rows of fruit trees show how the spot teems with culture on its sunny slope.   A light mantle of snow had fallen among the hills the morning this view was taken, and no trace of a foot-step was visible on the ground gone over that day.

In marked contrast was the appearance of the place and the way to it in mid-winter to the aspect they bore

in summer. The journey under a bright sky and a warm
air was enlivened by the song of birds, the darting of a

 squirrel, or the form of
a peasant in pursuit of
his daily avocation of
life; but there w a s
nought to break the
monotony of the cold
drive now. The sturdy
yeomanry were seeking
warmth by the fire that
lacked strength to thaw
the ice on a frost-coated
pane; all animal life
were housed, except a lone cow, that, sheltered by a
stack, twirled her cud of contentment in shivering
seclusion.

While Hartford was bleak and dismal for the want
of snow, the peaks and tips up near the hill were
inviting in their garb of crisp white. Winter in this
section strongly resembles the same season among the
foot-hills on the eastern slope of the Alleghany
Mountains. The cabin that clings to the side hill, and
the stream that tumbles through the gorge, are almost
one and the same. At the hill, all things were clothed
in a fleecy covering of pure white. The tops of fences
glistened in the weak winter sun, while the footstools
at the base of each cross had a soft, downy cushion of

THE BENEVOLENT HOME IN THE GORGE.   (See page 49.)

snow. An intense quiet brooded over all; not a sound
to break the day-dream of silence, except the whiff of
the ever-present wind as it industriously gathered
myriads of white particles from a peak to bury them
in some notch. The entire absence of life, the ominous
loneliness of the spot, combined with the clean, unpol-
luted look of every snow-laden tree, bush and twig,
impressed the beholder with a sense of the sanctity, and
purity of the place. It called up the lines:

> "Alone, and yet not all alone,
> I am with Him, and He's with me."

Such surroundings require but a moment of sincere
contemplation to place a man close to his Creator and
teach him his own utter insignificance.

From the place where the foot-path joins the road,
the rise is steep, with abrupt turns, and it requires a
good horse to draw a light buggy up the incline. The
approach is from the rear of the church to the right,
over a series of foot-hills to the gorge, which is still quite
a distance from the summit. Above the gorge a crooked
old path turns to the left as a short-cut. This is the
pathway first defined by the feet of the hermit, and
for years was the only way. The first close view of the
church is from a sharp bend some fifty feet lower than
the entrance, as the tired pedestrian toils wearily to the
left; and as it looms abruptly out of the clouds, his
weary feeling is mingled with surprise, and astonishment—surprise that an edifice of such pretensions should

have been erected in a place so inaccessible to the multitude from whom it was likely to derive support; and astonishment that so stupendous an undertaking could be successfully consumated upon a basis of faith alone. Faith that in the hearts of the people there was sufficient veneration for the spot to preserve its sanctity and insure its completion. A debt of eighteen thousand dollars to stare the staid, sober and well-intentioned people in the face, and nothing but voluntary contributions to pay it! Think of this, ye skeptics, who measure everything by the dollars and cents in sight, and tell me if the mysteries of the place are common.

If the aim of the founders was to erect this church in a place least likely to be susceptible to worldly influences, they have chosen a spot most appropriate. The climb extends to within five feet of the door-way, as the structure is upon the very summit of the knob. It is a plain, neat, brick building, of modern architecture, ornamented with double stone caps on the projecting corners and sides, Gothic windows, and surmounted with a substantial wooden belfry, tipped with a gold cross.

As I paused to note the singularity of the location, I realized the strange features of the spot. The close cut shadows at the base of the church wall told the hour of high noon; yet the only sound to interrupt a death-like stillness was the quaking leaves of the branches near me, swaying gently with a summer breeze. As I

THE PATH FROM THE MEADOW—WINTER SCENE.

mused on the solitude of the place, and the solemnity of the theme, I listened to the mournful cadence of the night wind, whispering to the latticed belfry a tale of romance that will ever cling to the place with traditional persistency. Dreaming, I peered through the dim mist of a past half century, to the night the crippled hermit crawled through the thick wood to this isolated peak. In the gathering gloom of a cold autumn eve' I beheld the bent form of the recluse, weak from illness and exhaustion, dragging his palsied limbs over rocks and tough undergrowth, to this lonely peak in the wilderness, to pay the penalty of an early sin.

Surely mere faith could not sustain a being under such circumstances. Only inspiration or a great revealed truth could buoy him up to consumate such a herculean task. Indirectly, the romance of his life was instrumental in rededicating this hill to a holy purpose. Had he not become an anchorite, the musty old manuscript would have mouldered to dust in the oblivion of a convent, and this story, with its faults, untold.

A certain elation pervades the mind of a being after attaining a height to which he is entirely unaccustomed. There is a buoyancy of spirits, an exaltation, that fits him to admire his surroundings. Besides, an inherent perception teaches that all blessings come from above. We are prone to look up to the blue firmament as the home of the angels. The soothing power of peace and the fire of inspiration alike emanate from the same

unfathomable space.   Alone in this space, and fixed as
the stars that twinkle over it, the spire holds compan-

ionship with the clouds
that incessantly change.
Immovable among the
unrealities it is encircled
by the shadowy forms
of a spiritual existence.
It drips with d e w or
flashes back the sheen
of frost.   It can tran-
quily note the dying
flicker of a low cabin
light, yet is there to reflect the first beam of a bright
morning sun.   While its solitude appalls, its loneliness
makes a prominent mark for the shafts of capricious
elements, and when the tempests of heaven in fury
break over this cross of gold, the spirit that rides on the
storm will gather the prayers from the altar.

The church spire is on the end, over the main
entrance of double doors, which open under a circular
gallery, attached by the ends to both sides of the church.
The interior is cheerful, and well-lighted by the tall
windows of stained glass, whose varied colors tend to
give a subdued illumination to the chapel.   The dome
or roof is supported by six sanded columns, whose
slender proportions increase the height and beauty of the

A CLOSE VIEW OF THE CHURCH.   (See page 54.)

place. The chancel is nicely carpeted, and separated from the chapel by a low, latticed communion rail of wood, covered with dark cloth, extending across to narrow passageways on each side. In the chancel there are one main and two side altars. The combined cost of the three altars was eleven hundred dollars, and was contributed by persons interested in the welfare of the church. Back of the *mensa*, and projecting from underneath the canopy of the main altar, stands the tabernacle or receptacle of the blessed sacrament, built in accordance with the rules of Catholic architecture, having a double door, with lock and key, nicely ornamented in gold with grapes and heads of wheat, the emblems of the blessed sacrament. Underneath and in front of the *mensa* is a figure of the Lamb of God resting on a sealed book. The candelabra, and many of the accessories pertaining to the faith, were also the gifts of charitably disposed persons.

The vestry room is a low addition on the rear and side, close to the bluff that overlooks the valley, with its farms and improvements, hundreds of feet below. The main body of the interior is still in an unfinished condition. There are nothing but low, crude, plank seats, without backs, laid upon cut blocks, for the worshipers to rest upon; but even these must bring a sigh of relief to some of the tired toilers of the hill.

To the right in the chancel, suspended from the side wall, hangs a square case, with glass front, entitled a "votive tablet ". In this a part of the sacred relics of the shrine are preserved. Among the vow offerings inclosed are three pairs of spectacles, left here as proofs of the efficacy of the place in the restoration of sight to those whose vision had been impaired by disease.

There are also stored, generally in some nook or window recess, a number of well-worn crutches. They are the accumulation of years, and were left by pilgrims whose infirmities were removed by the invisible power that controls the weird destiny of the place.

INTERIOR VIEW OF THE CHURCH. (See page 54.)

PART SIXTH.

Some of the Cures.

Taking life's pathway through,
Think how little we know
    Of the load that our neighbor must bear !
We're inclined to be bright,
If our burden is light,
    Yet we'd sink with the half he could spare.

THE writer originally intended to dispense with the details of the perfected cures, but an expressed desire on the part of some who admired the subject, led him to vary a little from his plan, and give the history of a few well-authenticated cases. Still he has no inclination to mar the beauty of the work by loading it, like a patent medicine pamphlet, with voluminous testimonials.

The list of cures, as compiled by competent authority, includes Saint Vitus' dance, epilepsy, ophthalmia, paralysis, rheumatism, melancholy, cancer, stiffness of limbs, and acute sufferings in other forms.

For thirty years this place has been accumulating the catalogue, and while the most of those interviewed speak enthusiastically, a few are reticent who claim to be the recipients of great relief.

Chicago *Tribune* special, speaking of this place, says :
" During the course of my investigations as to the traditions of the hill, in the line of miracles, I made the
acquaintance of an intelligent German farmer, Matt.
Werner, who has kept for years a sort of public house,
at which great numbers of religious pilgrims have
stopped during their sojourn at the hill, and he has had
an excellent opportunity to inform himself as to the
truth of their stories. He is himself a zealous, though
not a bigoted Catholic, and a man of excellent repute
among his neighbors. The following is his statement of
a few cures, as nearly in his own language as possible :

Cure A: " Louis Marms, of Hartford, was the first
man I knew to be cured on the hill. When he came
there he had no use of his limbs below the knee, but
went on crutches. He went on the hill every day, and
one day a lady came into my house and asked two
neighbors who were there to go up the hill and help
the poor man down, as he was very bad and could not
kneel, sit, or lie down, and that he was crying out with
pain all the time. I was laid up in bed, and the neighbors were playing cards with me. Before we had finished
our game we heard some one singing and shouting, and
looking out saw Marms coming along on one crutch
and swinging the other in his hand. The next day he
left one crutch at the church, and the following day left
the other and walked with a cane only. I said to him

then I could not believe he had been as bad off as he
pretended.   At this the tears came in his eyes, and he
showed me his limbs and his feet, which were nothing
but skin and bone.   This was several years ago, and
since that time Marms has become entirely well, and is
a big, heavy, healthy man.   He recently kept a store
at Hartford, where he was known as 'Cheap John.' "

Cure B : " In 1881 an Englishman, who kept a
hotel in La Salle, Ill., came and stopped with me for a
while.   He was seventy or eighty years old, and bald-
headed, but he would go up on the hill, in the hot sun,
without any hat.   He said that before he came to the
hill he could not be out in the sun on a hot day without
having a terrible headache.   He could run about here
bare-headed till his head was blistered, but had no pain.
He was a Protestant when he came, but became a
Catholic."

Cure C : " I have heard, Mr. Werner, of a case
of a child that could not walk, and never had walked a
step, that was brought by the mother to the hill at the
age of five years.   My informant says that one day
when the mother was sitting on a bench in the church,
another lady kneeling at some distance, dropped her
handkerchief, whereupon the child slid off her mother's
lap, and, walking over, picked it up.   He says he saw
that himself.   Do you know anything about it ? "   I

asked. " Yes, sir," he answered. " I saw it, too. It is true."

Cure D: In the town of Richfield, less than two miles south of Miracle Hill, and close to the St. Augustine church property, is the residence of Mr. John George Merkel. In the year 1882, Mr. Merkel was seriously afflicted with what proved to be a cancer of a malignant type. For two years it baffled all medical skill, and continued to eat away his nose and face. Besides the prescriptions given by physicians, he used all the domestic remedies known and suggested by those interested in his case, without in the least retarding the encroachments of the fell disease. Having been prepared for death by the priest, he shrank from the operation to be performed by a surgeon's knife, and as a last resource he had recourse to Miracle Hill. His cure seeming beyond the pale of doubt, and his time on earth short, he took a vow to make a pilgrimage to the hill, and repeat a certain prayer, every evening of his few remaining days. Strange to relate after the fulfillment of his resolution, for a short time, the ravages of the cancer apparently began to abate. Sustained by an additional hope of a cure, he now unfalteringly journeyed to the summit of the peak, and racked his brain for expedients to add to the sincerity of his devotion. After the lapse of two years his health was entirely restored, and now, at the age of seventy-seven, he is able to perform the duties of a stone mason. Elizabeth Merkel, his wife, testifies to the above facts.

Cure E: Miss Clara Krœger, daughter of Casper Krœger, 416 Mineral Street, Milwaukee, Wis., had been afflicted with a disease peculiar to the eye, known as ophthalmia, until she was almost blind. She had been under the treatment of an eminent occulist for two years without a sign of relief or hope of a cure. Her father had heard of the wonderful cures perfected by a sojourn at Miracle Hill, and believed that his daughter, who was then twelve years of age, could be benefited by a pilgrimage to the place. He had instilled her with his belief and she became convinced of its efficacy. Thither the father and daughter journeyed on a bright day in June, 1886, and on the morning of the day on which they ascended the hill, the girl was obliged to use artificial means to open her eyes. Father and daughter climbed the rugged slope, hand-in-hand, praying for relief as they toiled to the summit of the peak, the daughter making the vows or promises usual among those of her faith, and the father sustaining her by the wisdom of his counsel. They were there but one day, but she left her glasses in the church. The following morning she had no trouble in opening her eyes, or in seeing everything. The father returned home with her apparently as well as ever. She immediately resumed her studies at school, completely cured, nor has she ever experienced any trouble with her eyesight since. Both the father and daughter, through a spirit of gratitude, make a pilgrimage once a year to the sacred place to renew their vows, and by their devotion give a manifestation of thankfulness. The young lady is just budding into womanhood now. Her father is the junior partner in the well known dry-goods house of "Krœger Brothers" of this city.

Cure F: Mr. A. Scherrer, of New Munster, Wis., while shooting squirrels, August 25th, 1887, met with a serious accident, which threatened for a time to destroy his sight. The breech-pin of a muzzle-loading gun blew out with the discharge and the powder filled his eyes and face. The right eye, being open to sight the weapon, received the burning charge, causing the most intense pain. After two weeks close attention the physician declared his inability to give him relief, and advised a consultation with a well-known occulist in the City of Milwaukee. After submitting to an operation by one skilled in his calling, he was, for three months, a victim of great suffering, which continued almost without cessation. In the latter part of the following July and August he was again under treatment in the city, with no abatement of the acute misery, except when the eye was under the influence of an anæsthetic that made him oblivious to its intensity for a few hours, after which it returned with increased severity, when he would suffer untold agony. In this condition he was at last induced to visit Miracle Hill. I give the cure in his own words: "The first time I went up the hill I was unable to observe any relief, but the next day, while in the chapel of the church, the pain left me. Since then it has not returned and I can see and bear the light which I could not endure before."

Cure G: The case of Miss Ida M. Klingle, of Burlington, Wis., aged 21, was the only cure that came under the immediate observation of the writer. She was the one lone occupant of the deserted chapel on a bright day in June, 1887, and the first time he ever looked into the interior of the Miracle Hill church. She had suffered acutely with weak and inflamed eyes a number of years and had been under medical treatment for months just previous to making her appearance here, without the least apparent relief. When she arrived at the house in the gorge her eyes were carefully protected from the strong light by a visor and bandage and she was unable to see any object distinctly. She was an incessant visitor at the church, and less than one week after her arrival, served a dinner for two of us in the little log farm-house in the valley, flitting to and from the out-kitchen, in the hot sun, without hat, visor or bandage, and she read the fine print of a newspaper, when handed to her, readily.

Perhaps the most potent error that could be

indulged in by those in doubt of the efficacy of this place, would be to assume that there was no foundation of facts to rest these marvelous cures upon. An eminent physician of New York says: " Every competent physician, who has had to deal with mental troubles, knows perfectly well that the influence of the mind upon the body is something to be counted upon as of the utmost value as a therapeutical adjuvant, and scores of men owe their eminence in the profession to their faculty of influencing the minds of their patients for good."

Adversity is the test of man's fortitude, yet no man, however self-willed, but becomes pliant under the weight of a deep affliction. True, a woman, naturally weak, may be strong under the pressure of vicissitude. She lives upon inspirational power—the daughters of Hope, Sympathy and compassion will sustain her by the influence that mind exerts over body.

Being creatures of circumstances we are susceptible to invisible influences that change the tenor of our existence. A trifling circumstance—like the bars of a switch—may send our train a thousand miles in an opposite direction.

In scanning the horizon of facts for a basis to rest these cures upon, so many and varied theories arise that it is hard to solve the problem, and meet the criticism of public opinion.

One beauty of the Catholic religion is its faith in the

power of prayer; and this church is based upon that belief. To those who lack that faith, the theory of mind cure offers the only solution of the question to be solved. That the mind exercises a strange influence over the body, for good or evil, no one can doubt; and these miracles may be largely attributable to the restoration of lost powers by complete quiet, and diversion of the mind from all perplexing annoyances existing elsewhere.

The sojourner here is lost to all outside influences. He is encircled by the weird beliefs that cluster around the entire neighborhood, and lulled to rest by the uninterrupted harmony that pervades it. He meets with sympathy and is buoyed by hope. No doubts or dissentions, as to the infallibility of the place, mar the quiet of his stay. All these, combined with wholesome food, pure air, and incomparably beautiful surroundings, must and will accomplish marvelous results.

www.ingramcontent.com/pod-product-compliance
Lightning Source LLC
Chambersburg PA
CBHW030018030726
47499CB00008B/3039